W9-BBZ-464

The Far-Flung Adventures of
Homer the Hummer

by Cynthia Furlong Reynolds • Illustrations by Catherine McClung

mitten press

Sometimes the smallest and most ordinary-looking creatures have the biggest and most extraordinary adventures. Homer, a ruby-throated hummingbird no bigger than your index finger, is one of the world's great travelers. His life is full of danger, daredevil stunts, and distant lands.

One of Homer's greatest adventures begins within the Monteverde cloud forest of Costa Rica. Beneath a canopy of dark green trees, birds of every color, size, and shape chirp for attention and compete for food. They soar, swoop, sashay, glide, glean, or grub while calling, clamoring, chattering, cheering, singing, screeching, screaming, pecking, poking, and preening. In their midst, a tiny little creature with impossibly fast-moving wings darts among tropical blooms.

Homer loves the sugary sweetness found in intense red, pink, and purple flowers. He buzzes up to a bloom, hovers in the air, and sticks his long beak and even longer tongue into its trumpet. He sips the nectar, backs away, hovers, then flies to another flower to sip again. And again. In between meals, he rests on a tiny branch, alert for snacks. He is particularly fond of juicy mosquitoes, grayish gnats, frisky fireflies, and tiny, scrambling spiders. Other birds may be more powerful, more colorful, or more musical, but a hummingbird is the greatest of gymnasts. This is the only bird in the world able to hover and fly forward, backward, even upside down.

In mid-March, Homer prepares for his great homeward journey, which will take him six hundred miles across the Gulf of Mexico, then hundreds of miles up through the eastern United States. To fly so far and so fast, Homer must eat all the right foods and lots of them. For days on end, he eats. And eats. And eats. Then, early one morning, when a warm northbound tailwind begins to blow, Homer sips from one last flower and soars

up...

...up...

...and away!

Up and down! Up and down! Those tiny wings keep moving. Blue-gray, sparkling water and rolling waves stretch to the horizon in every direction as Homer flies high above the great, wide water. Out there, he will find no branches for resting, no flowers for feeding.

Homer flies. And he flies. And he flies some more.

Gradually, he drops lower and lower, until he barely skims the waves. Just when it seems that those wings can't possibly continue to move, Homer sights land. With one last gasp, the exhausted little bird zips across the shoreline.

Like a dive-bomber, he heads for his target: brilliant red impatiens along the edge of a quiet pond.

He eats. And he eats. Then colors dazzle his eyes as he swoops down to misty water. After a refreshing bath, Homer will continue his gourmet meal.

A big green frog hopes to do the same. Eyes wide and unblinking, the frog sits motionless on a nearby rock until Homer shakes his feathers dry. Suddenly, a long, sticky tongue shoots in Homer's direction.

With a startled Buzz! Homer scrambles backward into the air, breathless and fright-ened, barely escaping. He zooms across the pond and buries himself in a mass of bright blooms. But now he keeps a sharp lookout for those who might be interested in hummingbird dinners.

The world is a far, far different place when viewed from the basket of a hot-air balloon. Homer peers down at a patchwork panorama of farms, forests, and rivers stretching far below him. The enormous floating mass of color had attracted Homer's eyes, but when he fails to find a bonanza of sweet, sugary nectar, he continues on his journey. Mountains serve as his map as he flies.

Homer flies. And he flies. And he flies some more.

A balloon might not offer nectar, but a farm stand overflowing with fragrant, flamboyant flowers offers a smorgasbord of fine dining. When the sun begins to cool, he forgets his meal and worriedly surveys the sky. The night air is cold, too cold.

Early the next morning, a small boy points to what might be a droopy leaf.

"Grandpa! Look! What's hanging up there?"

"It's a hummingbird!" the man says, gently detaching Homer from his perch. "He's as stiff as if he were carved out of bone and feathers." As the boy anxiously watches, his grandfather softly massages the little bird. But there is no sign of life.

"We'll bury him in Grandma's flowerbed," the man tells the boy. He carefully slips the hummingbird into his breast pocket and the two head for home. Grandpa feels a curious sensation on his chest.

He quickly steers off the road and reaches into his pocket— just as Homer becomes warm enough to continue on his way. The hummingbird buzzes in front of the startled man's nose as if to say, "Thanks!" Then he zooms out the window.

"What happened?" the boy asks, amazed.

"Apparently, that bird was in a deep sleep called torpor and he woke up," the man says, watching Homer soar into the sky.

Several days later, as a long, cool spring afternoon quietly draws to an end, an aging tractor leaves a field, heads down a lane, and veers into an old red barn. The bright red-orange sign on the tractor catches a hungry Homer's eye.

Homer follows the tractor, unbeknownst to the farmer, who closes the barn door and heads to his warm kitchen and hot dinner. When the sign offers no sweet nectar, Homer frantically searches for something else. But there is no food for him anywhere in the dark, dusty barn.

The next morning, soon after the rooster sings his wake-up call, the farmer discovers Homer lying beside the tractor. He stoops and scoops up the tiny, limp body, then rushes to nestle the hummingbird in a big pot of purple petunias hanging on his porch. Minutes later, Homer begins a very large, very long breakfast.

For several days, he doesn't stray far from his flowerpot and his friend. Then one noon, Homer circles around the farmer, flicks his tail, and soars into the sky.

Homer flies. And he flies. And he flies some more.

When the hills start rolling in a familiar way, Homer knows that he is nearing his journey's end. He flaps his wings harder than ever as he swoops and darts along a narrow, twisting lane and into the fragrant English-style garden he knows and loves.

As if to say, "Yoohoo! I'm home again!" Homer buzzes the artist's large kitchen window overlooking lilacs budding in Homer's garden.

"Homer! You're early this year! You made fine time," the artist says as she pours a sugar-water solution into the bright red hummingbird feeder.

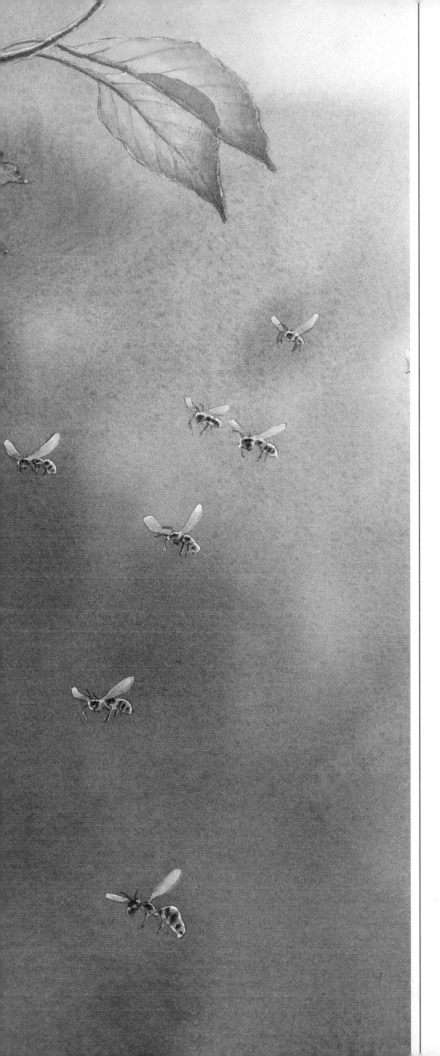

In the next few days, the orioles discover Homer's feeder and the little bird must wait in line for a chance to sip the sugary water. Later, columns of hungry ants and swarms of buzzing bees also invite themselves to dinner. Every once in awhile, Homer is too hungry to wait politely; he flies to a nearby tree and feasts on bugs and sap dripping from holes drilled by a yellow-bellied sapsucker.

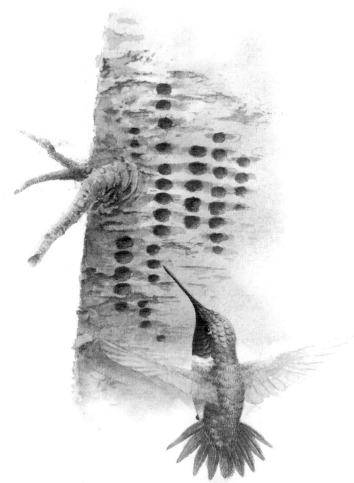

One morning, Ruby the Hummer appears at the end of her long migration from the south. Homer welcomes his sweetheart with his best aerial acrobatics. Homer soars and zooms in high-speed dives, then buzzes back and forth in front of Ruby.

"He looks like a pocket watch on an imaginary chain," the artist whispers. Later, Ruby begins to build. She is a perfectionist. Back and forth she flies,

collecting gentle things to make her nest.
Ruby lays two eggs, then climbs atop to
sit for nearly three weeks. When two tiny
chicks poke their heads over the top of
their walnut-sized nest, they catch the
first glimpse of their homeland.

After that, Ruby flies back and forth,
bringing food to her hungry babies. When
their feathers are formed, Ruby teaches
them the fine art of flying.

Summer tiptoes into the garden. Bushes and plants celebrate with fireworks of color. One afternoon, the artist sets her easel in the midst of snapdragons, scarlet sage, nasturtiums, bee-balm, sweet William, columbine, delphinium, and hollyhocks. Homer poses for his portrait as he feeds on sweet lunch.

Intrigued by the artist's paints, Homer hovers so close that the artist can feel the breeze from his wings on her face. "Mr. Audubon called your feathers 'glittering fragments of the rainbow'—and he was right," she says, admiring the way the sunshine glistens on Homer's tiny feathers.

One day, a little girl appears in Homer's garden. "This is my favoritest dress in the whole world because of the buttons," she tells the artist. Homer glimpses the cherries painted on those buttons and zooms over to admire them, hoping for a new sweet treat.

"Oh!" the little girl gasps, half in alarm, half in delight, as the miniature bird hums and buzzes under her chin.

"Hold very still," the artist whispers. "He won't hurt you. He just loves your buttons as much as you do!"

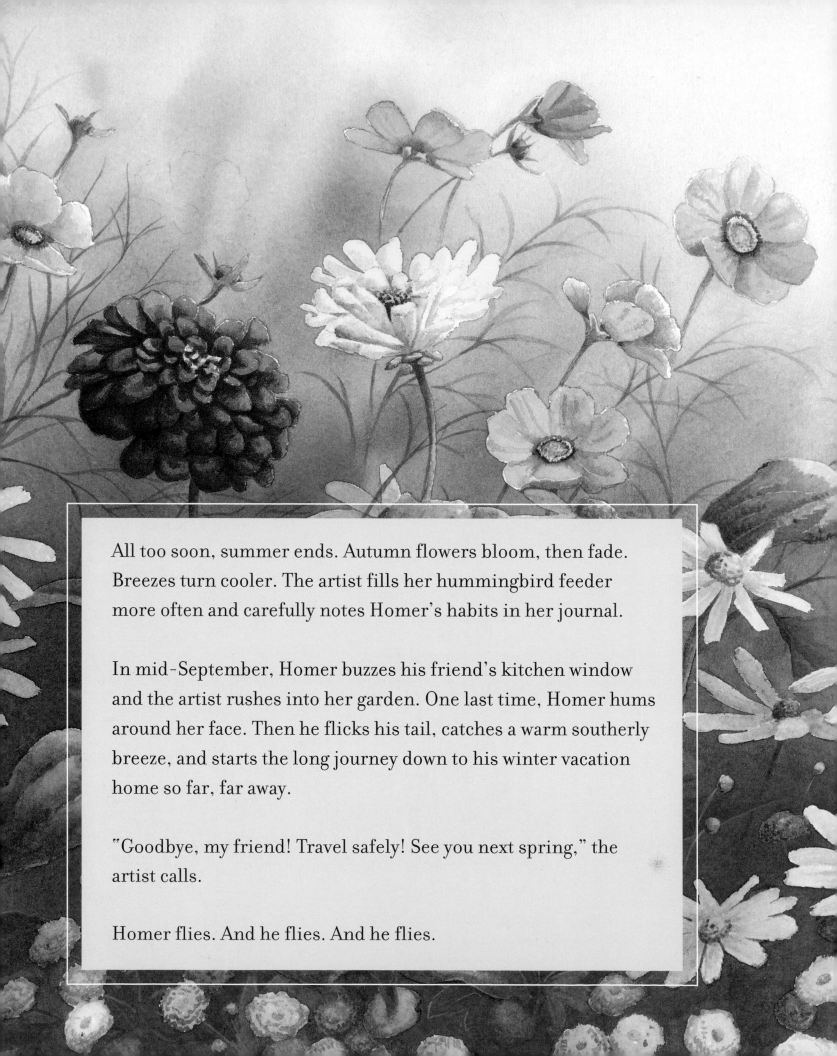

All too soon, summer ends. Autumn flowers bloom, then fade. Breezes turn cooler. The artist fills her hummingbird feeder more often and carefully notes Homer's habits in her journal.

In mid-September, Homer buzzes his friend's kitchen window and the artist rushes into her garden. One last time, Homer hums around her face. Then he flicks his tail, catches a warm southerly breeze, and starts the long journey down to his winter vacation home so far, far away.

"Goodbye, my friend! Travel safely! See you next spring," the artist calls.

Homer flies. And he flies. And he flies.

Did You Know?

The Western Hemisphere is home to 338 species of hummingbirds. Sixteen species can be found in the United States. Homer's type, the ruby-throated, is the third smallest of the 16, but the second most populous in the United States. These birds can be found in 41 states and 11 of the 12 Canadian provinces.

The tiny birds migrate as far as 2,500 miles, often across open water, twice each year—an extraordinary accomplishment. All of Homer's adventures in the book are based on stories of hummingbird behavior reported by amateur ornithologists throughout the United States.

Text Copyright © 2005 Cynthia Furlong Reynolds

Illustrations Copyright © 2005 Catherine McClung

All inquiries should be addressed to:

Mitten Press

An imprint of Ann Arbor Media Group LLC

2500 S. State Street

Ann Arbor, MI 48104

Printed and bound in Canada

09   08   07   06   05   1   2   3   4   5

Library of Congress Cataloging in Publication data on file.

ISBN 10: 1-58726-269-X

ISBN 13: 978-1-58726-269-2